There's No Nest Like Home

by Janelle Cherrington
illustrated by the Thompson Bros.

Simon Spotlight/Nickelodeon
New York   London   Toronto   Sydney   Singapore

Discovery Facts

Australian Outback: The area that makes up most of Australia's inland, or nearly 85 percent of its total landmass. Not many people live there because it is hot and very dry. Pockets of water can be found throughout this wild region, but they are few and far between.

Emu: Native to Australia and New Zealand, the emu is the second largest bird in the world. The emu cannot fly—but it can run up to forty-eight miles per hour! Because they don't fly, emus build their nests on the ground, usually in the trunks of fallen trees. But unlike many other birds, it is the emu father who cares for his young chicks. He has to work very hard because, along with berries and other fruit, an emu can eat up to 3,000 caterpillars a day!

KLASKY CSUPO INC.

Based on the TV series *The Wild Thornberrys*® created by Klasky Csupo, Inc. as seen on Nickelodeon®

SIMON SPOTLIGHT
An imprint of Simon & Schuster Children's Publishing Division
1230 Avenue of the Americas, New York, New York 10020

Copyright © 2000 Viacom International Inc. All rights reserved. NICKELODEON, *The Wild Thornberrys*, and all related titles, logos, and characters are trademarks of Viacom International Inc. All rights reserved including the right of reproduction in whole or in part in any form. SIMON SPOTLIGHT and colophon are registered trademarks of Simon & Schuster. Manufactured in the United States of America.
First Edition   2 4 6 8 10 9 7 5 3 1   ISBN 0-689-83385-7

"You'll have to watch Donnie today," Debbie said to Eliza as their parents left for a day of filming in the Australian Outback. "I've been getting E-mails from an Australian girl who told me where to look for this *amazing* clay that's perfect for mud masks!"

"I can see how finding mud to rub on your face is *much more important* than watching Donnie," Eliza said. "Anyway, we're going to look for kangaroos. Enjoy your dirt hunting."

As Eliza, Darwin, and Donnie walked into the Outback, Debbie headed for the riverbank. It didn't take her long to find a nice puddle of rich, black clay, just where her friend had said it would be!

"Yes!" Debbie shouted as she tested the mud.

Just then, something caught her eye. Sitting in a patch of sand near the riverbank was a large, funny-looking rock. Debbie didn't believe her eyes at first, but when she looked again, she realized the rock was moving—all on its own!

Just as Debbie bent down to get a closer look, the "rock" broke in two—and out popped a baby bird!

"Ew!" she said. "I thought baby birds were supposed to be cute."

"Peep! Peep! Peep!" the little chick answered as it looked up at Debbie with instant love.

"Why are you *looking* at me like that?" Debbie asked nervously. She looked around. Maybe she could find a nest and put the chick back. The egg couldn't have come from very far away.

As Debbie scanned the branches above her head, the little chick tottered to its feet and teetered alongside her.

Debbie didn't see a nest anywhere—but the thought of a nest reminded her that she hadn't brought a container for her mud. She looked down at the chick.

"Listen, bird," she said, "I don't know where you came from, but I think you'd better go find your parents. I'm leaving now, so uh, take care of yourself."

Then Debbie turned and walked away.

But the baby bird knew just what to do.

"Peep! Peep!" he said happily as he wobbled awkwardly behind her.

"Stop following me!" Debbie snapped. "Go home!"

When the chick didn't stop, Debbie started to run.

The bird just wobbled faster. He followed Debbie all the way back to the Commvee!

"Bird, what do you want?" Debbie asked. She didn't know how to make it go away.

"Peep!" the little chick answered hopefully.

"Eliza!" Debbie yelled at the top of her lungs. Where was her sister when she needed her?

"Jeez, Deb, what's going on?" Eliza asked when she arrived. Debbie pointed to the peeping chick. "It hatched right in front of me and now it won't go away! What does it *want* from me, Eliza?" Eliza started to giggle. "I have bad news for you, Deb. That's an emu chick, and he thinks you're his father."

"What?" Debbie shrieked. "Why would he think that?"

"Because you were the first thing he saw when he hatched," Eliza explained. "Emus are normally raised by their fathers. And Debbie, I think he's hungry."

"All I wanted to do today was get that mud," Debbie said, looking at the chick in frustration. "I don't even know what emus eat!"

"Caterpillars," Eliza replied. "Lots and lots of caterpillars."

"That's *disgusting*," Debbie said. "Can't you do it, Eliza?"

"Sorry, Deb. I think he'll only take them from you," Eliza said.

"Oh, all right already!" Debbie cried as she grabbed a bucket from the Commvee and trudged into the Outback. "But you'd better think of *something* to get me out of this mess while I'm gone."

Debbie didn't have any trouble finding caterpillars. She found a nest of fat, hairy, wiggly ones in the first place she looked. Her problem was figuring out how to get them in the bucket without actually touching them.

First she tried pointing at them. "Eat up. Yum, yum!" she said.

But the emu just stared at Debbie and peeped.

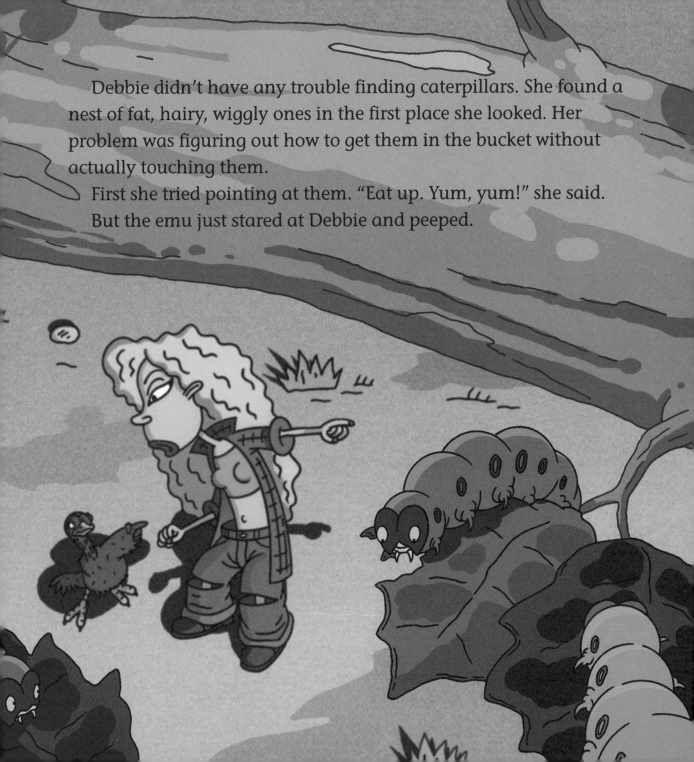

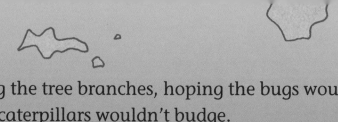

Next Debbie tried shaking the tree branches, hoping the bugs would fall into her bucket. But the caterpillars wouldn't budge.

Debbie knew that her worst fears had come true. She would have to pick the caterpillars off the tree with her fingers!

"Yuck! Yuck! Yuck!" Debbie said, squirming as she dropped them one by one into her bucket.

"Oh, that really *is* disgusting!" Darwin whispered to Eliza when he saw Debbie's wriggling collection.

"Eliza, are you sure emus eat caterpillars?" Debbie asked. "He doesn't seem to want them."

"Debbie, he hasn't ever eaten anything before," Eliza explained. "You have to *show* him how."

"That's it!" Debbie yelled. "If you think that I am going to *eat* a caterpillar to set an example for a bird, you've lost your mind!"

Suddenly, Donnie grabbed a caterpillar from the bucket and swallowed it whole.

"Donnie!" Eliza yelled.

But the baby emu finally understood! He ate the bucket clean in a flash—then looked at Debbie for more. He knew right then and there that caterpillars were the best things ever!

"He can't be hungry again," Debbie said with a tired sigh.

"I told you emus eat *lots* of caterpillars," Eliza said. "Why don't you go get more while I take the chick back to the riverbank. We obviously have to find his real father."

As soon as Debbie was gone, Eliza tried to explain the situation to the little chick. "I'm sorry but Debbie is *not* your father."

"I don't believe you," the chick replied.

"Think about it," Eliza reasoned. "You look nothing like her."

"She has two legs and a head," said the chick, "and she's the best dad in the whole wide world!"

"But she doesn't have wings or feathers or a beak," Eliza continued. "And she *hates* caterpillars."

Meanwhile, Darwin had spotted the emu father. The big bird was sitting on a nest in an upturned tree stump. "Excuse me, but I think I have something that belongs to you," Eliza said to the adult bird. "Your son."

"No son of mine would even be seen with a human," the emu father replied. "I'm afraid you're mistaken. Now go away."

"But every other animal in the Outback told us this was the handsomest chick they'd ever seen," Eliza said in her most sincere voice. "And they swore you looked exactly like him when you were young. They said you just *had* to be his father."

"Well, now that you mention it," the father said, "I do see a certain resemblance."

"Me too," the baby agreed. "But do you like caterpillars?"

"Naturally!" the adult emu replied. "Who doesn't like caterpillars?"

"Dad!" the chick cried as he wobbled over to the nest.

"Welcome home, son," the father said.

Eliza and Darwin returned to the Commvee to tell Debbie the good news. "I solved your problem, Deb. As we speak, that chick is nesting happily with his *real* father. You can thank me later," Eliza said.

"Yeah, right. Thanks for not telling me *before* I collected these caterpillars!" Debbie replied.

But when Debbie finally made it back to the riverbank for her mud, she made one more stop. After all, there was no sense in wasting all those disgusting caterpillars.